Richard III

Written by William Shakespeare

Retold by Chris Powling

Illustrated by Davide Ortu

Collins

Characters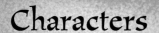

Lord Stanley – an old soldier, related to the Earl of Richmond

Queen Elizabeth – wife of King Edward IV, and mother of the young Prince Edward and Prince Richard

Earl of Richmond – Son-in-law of Lord Stanley, he goes on to become King Henry VII

Prince Edward and Prince Richard – the two young princes, sons of King Edward IV and Queen Elizabeth and nephews of Richard, Duke of Gloucester

King Edward IV – Richard's older brother, who's king when the story begins

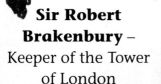

Sir Robert Brakenbury – Keeper of the Tower of London

Lord Hastings – a faithful old friend of Richard's

Richard, Duke of Gloucester – eventually crowned King Richard III

Queen Margaret – widow of the previous king, Henry VI

Duke of Buckingham – Richard's right-hand man

George, Duke of Clarence – Richard's other brother

Princess Anne – daughter-in-law of the previous king, Henry VI, and widow of the king's son; she goes on to marry Richard

3

1 Richard and his brothers

Let's begin with Richard's shadow.

There it lay, flat against the castle flagstones, as sharp and black and sinister as Richard himself.

Notice its crooked back.

Examine its withered left hand.

They were ugly enough when Richard was standing still. Imagine how much worse they looked on the man himself as he skittered spider-like across the courtyard with that sly, sneering smile on his face.

As usual, knowing he was alone, he was thinking aloud. His crisp, high voice was enough in itself to send a shudder down your spine. Yet, somehow, for all its creepiness, every twisted inch of him reminded you he was royalty – the Duke of Gloucester, no less. He belonged to the House of York and his older brother Edward had just become king … King Edward IV of England. The House of Lancaster, their deadly enemy for more than 30 years, had just been defeated. The red rose of York had finally triumphed over the white rose of Lancaster. Enough to make any man happy, you'd think.

But not a man like Richard.

He ran his tongue over thin, bitter lips.
"Glorious summer at last," he hissed. "Our winter days are over. But now, in this tedious time of peace, how will I stop myself dying of boredom? After all, I can't dance. I can't sing. I can't jest with the ladies – not with a face and a body like mine. Why, if I bend down to pat a dog, it barks back at me in terror! Thank goodness – or do I mean thank badness – there's one thing my twisted shape's truly fit for: the deepest, darkest *villainy*."

Richard paused a moment to gloat. He hopped from one lame foot to the other like a bird of prey about to pounce. "No heart's as hard as mine and no brain as quick," he smirked. "I can run rings around the lot of them – not just that upstart, the Earl of Richmond, the House of Lancaster's last hope. No problem there. More to the point, I'm head and hump above my fellow Yorkists, too. My feeble brother, the king, for instance. Or my other brother, George, the Duke of Clarence. What a puff of nothing he is. The sooner I get rid of him the better. Is he really ahead of me in line to the throne? How ridiculous is that! I've already hatched a little plot to sort him out."

He broke off just in time. The sound of iron-shod feet rang out on the flagstones. Sir Robert Brakenbury, Keeper of the Tower of London, was striding towards him ahead of two heavily armed soldiers. Between the soldiers, looking baffled, was a richly dressed nobleman.

"Well, mercy me!" cried Richard. "If it isn't George himself!"

"My brother Richard!" George groaned. "Can you believe it? I'm under arrest … on my way to a dungeon in the tower!"

"A dungeon, Brother?"

"By orders of our eldest brother, the king, Edward himself! And all because … because – "

"Because of what, Brother?"

"Because my name begins with G."

"So it does … and always has done. You've been George since the day you were born. How can the king blame you for that? You were too young to object at the time."

"Richard, that's what I told him."

"And his answer?"

"I was wasting my breath. He's surrounded himself with wizards and fortune-tellers, and one of them predicted that somebody with the initial 'G' would take the throne away from his children. He's convinced himself it's me. So here I am – a prisoner!"

Richard lifted his withered hand. "Wizards, you say? Fortune-tellers? George, it's not those people you should blame. It's all the women the king's gathered round him – especially his wife, the new Queen Elizabeth. Remember how she sent the loyal Lord Hastings to jail for a while? She's worse than the Lancastrians! She wants to grab every last bit of the kingdom for herself and her friends. We're not safe, George. We're not safe – "

Richard swung round to face Sir Robert, Keeper of the Tower. "Did I hear you speak, Sir Robert?"

"I beg your pardon, my lords, but the king gave me orders that no one, however high in rank, should speak privately to my prisoner."

"Privately?" said Richard. He smiled his smoothest, silkiest smile. "Sir Robert, there's nothing private about this conversation. Feel free to listen to everything we say … the king's wise and good, his queen's old but still pretty and all her relatives have done very, very well for themselves since her husband came to the throne. Is that fair comment? Have I said anything to displease my brother King Edward?"

"No, your grace – "

"I'm so glad you agree. Goodbye for now, George. No, not another word. I'm off to see the king and set you free."

11

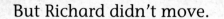

But Richard didn't move.

He stayed exactly where he was till the others were out of sight. "Wizards?" he said, raising an eyebrow. "Fortune-tellers? Luckily, they'll say anything if you pay them as much as I did. Poor King Edward. He won't live long, I hope. As for dumb, honest George, I love him so much I'll soon usher him out of this cruel, wicked world. He's much too nice for this place!"

He gave a lopsided skip for the fun of it. "Come on, shadow," he said. "You look so slick and so evil, you remind me of the person I care about most above all others. Now who's that, I wonder? Oh yes, it's *me*."

2 Richard seeks a bride

Picture an old, gloomy abbey lit by candles.
Under its soaring stonework and tall, dim windows,
lies a king in his coffin. He's waiting to be buried.
No, it's not Richard's sickly brother Edward.
He's still alive … at least for now. This is the former
king, Henry VI, the last king from the house of
Lancaster, who'd been stabbed bloodily to death.

And whose sword did the stabbing?

Can't you guess?

The same man also killed Henry's son. Just think:
father and son – two generations – both disposed of in
the battle between the red rose of York and the white
rose of Lancaster. It takes a hard heart and a quick
brain to do that. The heart and the brain of Richard,
Duke of Gloucester, for instance.

Even now, as he lurked in the shadows, he was plotting his next move. But he wasn't brooding over the dead king. His eyes were fixed on Henry's daughter-in-law, the Princess Anne, who was slumped against the coffin weeping for her husband and his royal father. "Beautiful," Richard murmured. "Quite beautiful. And I want her for my wife."

Had she heard him?

She leapt to her feet, her face smudged with tears. "You?" she gasped. "You? You toad! You viper! You devil! You snatched the lives of the men I loved. Are you here to steal their souls as well?"

"Sweet princess, don't be angry – "

"Angry?" Anne almost laughed. Instead, her choking sob of despair seemed to echo to the topmost arch of the abbey. "You destroyed them both," she wailed. "Do you deny that, you lump of foulness?"

"Dear lady, I admit it."

"What?"

"I killed the two of them," Richard sighed. "A double-murder for which I beg forgiveness whenever I say my prayers. I weep, on my knees, for the harm I did such noble, honourable men."

"*What?*"

"You don't believe that, I know. Just look at me … a poor wretch of a cripple with one hand no better than a claw. What forgiveness can I expect even from you, the best of women?"

"None, sir. Not the smallest glimmer. From me, *this* is what you can expect and what you deserve!" She curled her tongue and spat at him.

15

Richard's hooded eyes blinked once, just once. Slowly, he lifted the hand that was a claw to his face ... but not to wipe away the spittle. Instead, he caressed it tenderly as if it was a dab of the sweetest perfume. "It came from your mouth," he crooned. "The mouth I'd kiss so willingly – "

"A kiss from you?" Anne cried. "I'd rather kiss a rat or an adder or a hedgehog ridden with plague!"

"Nor would I blame you, madam."

"Blame me? The only blame here lies with the monster who ended two innocent lives for no good reason."

"For no good reason?" said Richard.

Anne stared at him in amazement. Did she actually see a tear run down his cheek? Was his chin really trembling like an infant in distress? And what had happened to his voice? She'd never heard it so soft and sorrowful. "The clash and clamour of battle was just my excuse, dear lady," he said, brokenly. "All's fair in war, they say. But all's fair in love as well. And love was the reason I killed your husband and his father."

"You murdered them out of *love*?"

"My love for you, Princess."

"For *me*?"

"Since the first instant I saw you. I fell for you at once from the crook on my back down to my turned-in toes. But now, alas, I see I've lost you for ever. So what have I left to live for?"

He stepped away from her and ripped open his shirt from neck to waist. Then, with his one good hand, he drew his sword. A flick of the wrist flipped it over in the air so its hilt was closest to Anne and its tip closest to him ... to his bare defenceless chest. "One lunge," he said. "One single lunge will bring you your revenge and rid me of my torment. Strike, lady."

She seized the weapon. She braced herself for the blow. "Don't spare me," came Richard's plea. "Think of their love, not mine."

"I can't," she sobbed.

The blade clattered on the abbey floor.

Richard looked at it a moment then back at Anne. "Take up the sword again," he said. "Or take me up."

She shook her head.

Suddenly, still crouching, he held the sword-tip against his throat. He tilted his chin a little as if to make the final jab as deadly as she could wish. "Then bid me kill myself," he said. "And I'll do it."

Again she shook her head. She was swaying on her feet now. Her eyes were blank with bewilderment. Was she astonished at the sheer cheek of this crumpled demon in front of her who seemed willing to break every rule? Was he really that strong, that fearless? How could anyone refuse such a … such a bundle of boldness, drive and energy?

Richard saw his chance. "So?" he asked. "Can I hope to achieve my heart's desire, at least one day?"

"Anyone can hope, I hope," she said.

"Then take this ring, sweet lady. Let it be a token of better things between us. In the meantime, you shouldn't linger here. Leave me to bury this noble king for you with every honour due to him."

"Gladly," said Anne, dully.

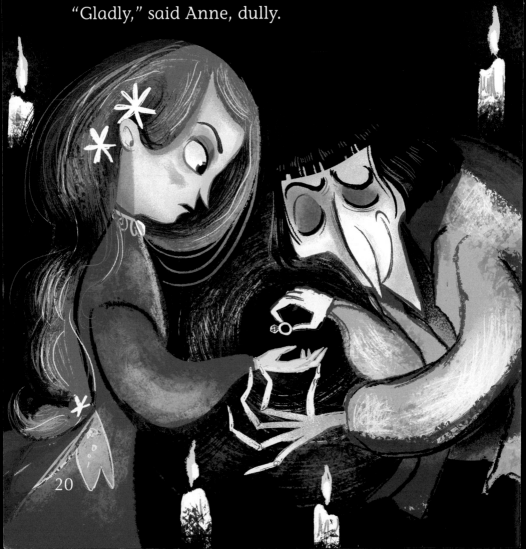

"Gladly," he repeated, when she was gone. "She'll be mine within the week – despite two corpses as my wedding gift. Mind you, I'll only keep her as long as it suits me. If I can win a bride as easily as this, what's to stop me winning the kingdom by and by?"

Carefully, he wiped his hook of a hand on the hangings of King Henry's coffin. "So what's next?" he smiled. "Oh, yes – disposing of a pair of brothers. I love them deeply, of course. But I'll love them all the better when they're as dead as this numpty in his wooden box."

3 The killing of brother George

George woke up in a sweat. He'd been dreaming of
a terrible storm at sea … and of Richard, his brother.
"I tried to save him," George croaked, "and, by
chance, he knocked me overboard! I sank like a stone,
down, down, down to an ocean graveyard littered
with bones. Is there any death worse than drowning?"
Shuddering, he pushed away the blankets. His gaze
fell on the walls of his prison, on the earth floor,
on the high window crisscrossed with iron bars.
His nostrils twitched at the dank smell all round him.
"But this is a nightmare, too," he groaned. "Help me,
Richard! Help me!"

"Help you, my lord?" came a hard, cold voice.
"Your wish is granted. That's exactly why we're here."

George shrank back.

How long had they been there, in the shadows,
these two hooded visitors in their rough working
clothes? Had they been watching him toss and turn
in terror? Had they heard his cries of panic? He licked
his lips. "Have you … have you come to kill me?"
he asked.

"To kill you, your grace?" the speaker went on.
"Now why would you think that? We're here to ease
your pain, that's all."

He jabbed his companion in the ribs. "Isn't that a fact?" he sniggered. "To ease his *pain*?"

"Something like that – " the second man sighed.

The first man, the hard, cold one, glared at him. "You goin' soft on me?" he snarled. "This is official business, right? We've got a proper warrant for it. Otherwise, they'd never have let us in here."

"A warrant?" said George, as he struggled to his feet. "May I see it, good fellow?"

No, you may not … good sir. It's for our eyes only, 'cept for the man who wrote it. Or maybe I mean for *my* eyes only – not for this coward standing next to me who's forgotten how much we're bein' paid!"

His partner shook his head. "I haven't forgotten it," he mumbled. "I've remembered my conscience, that's all. There's not enough money in the world to make up for losing that."

"Well said!" George exclaimed. "Show me the warrant, I beg. My brother King Edward isn't himself these days. His mind's wandering. If he was the one who wrote it – "

"Sorry, my old son. You're talkin' about the wrong brother. Richard's the one you should've been watching."

With a leer of hard, cold triumph, the taller and tougher of the visitors took a step forward as if to give George a friendly hug. But it wasn't a hug at all. It was a punch. A punch with a clenched fist – which held a short, sharp dagger in its grip.

George collapsed without a sound.

In one corner of the dungeon was
a chest-high barrel of water put there for
the comfort of royal prisoners. "Just what I need,"
the murderer growled. "He'll fit in that very nicely.
Now, what was it this duke feller said about drownin'
bein' the worst possible way for a man to die? Well,
he got lucky there, didn't he … 'cos I stabbed him *first*.
Now, are you goin' to help me or not?"

His partner turned away in horror.

4 A rumbling among royalty

It was a noble gathering round the sick King Edward's bed. Here were the grandest lords and ladies in the land – every one of them struck dumb by the look on Edward's face.

Dumb, did I say?

Queen Margaret, with her eerie cackle and vicious curses, wasn't dumb. As the widow of the previous king, Henry VI, she'd already lost her husband and son thanks to a certain royal duke who hadn't yet arrived – the one who cast such an *interesting* shadow.

Remember him?

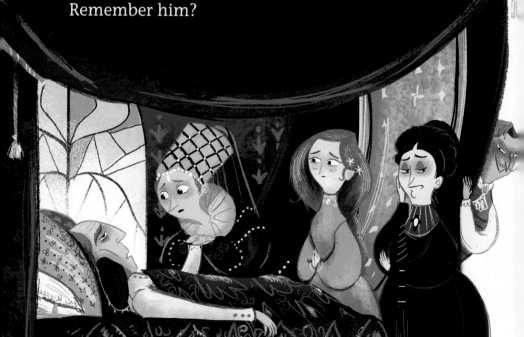

They should all have remembered him. They should all have listened to Mad Queen Margaret, too. "Richard! Richard! Richard!" she muttered. "If there's any evil to be done, we can rely on you to do it! Now I hear you want to marry my son's widow, Anne. Is there nothing you won't stoop to? Not that you need stoop very far with a shape like yours – "

King Edward lifted a feeble hand. His cheeks flushed and his voice trembling, he was poised halfway between life and death. He looked as if he knew it, too. "My lords and ladies," he wheezed. "Bring love to this kingdom, not hate. For my sake, treat each other like friends, not enemies. England's suffered enough from the wars between York and Lancaster. Now's the time for peace and forgiveness – "

"No hope of that," said Margaret to herself. "Not with that troll, that hobgoblin Richard around."

"Let me begin with my own brother, George," Edward continued. "I was told he was plotting against me and I sent him to the tower for punishment. Well, that was wrong. Today, I've set him free."

"Not free exactly, your majesty!"

Limping sideways like a crab, Richard had made his usual eye-catching entrance. "Has the news not reached you, Brother?" he frowned. "Better brace yourself for sorrow, then. Your pardon arrived too late."

"See what I mean?" sniffed Mad Old Margaret.

"Too late?" Edward gasped.

"George was found at the tower this morning drowned in a vat of water," Richard sighed. "I've warned him over and over again about guzzling such stuff when it's still fresh. He just wouldn't listen. Now, alas, it's the last thing he'll ever do."

"But not the last thing you'll ever do, you scorpion!" Mad Margaret spluttered.

"George is dead?" choked Edward. "Are you sure, dear Brother? Is there no chance of a mistake?"

"No chance at all, your majesty. I checked the matter myself. George is as dead as a door knocker – oh, mercy me! What a slip of the tongue! I should have said something more tactful – "

As if ashamed of himself, Richard hid his face behind his mangled hand.

Even Mad Margaret was shocked at such play-acting. "As dead as your own feelings," she hissed. "That's what you should've said."

Richard scuttled to the back of the room. King Edward lay flat on his back, with Elizabeth, his queen, fussing desperately over him. The other lords and ladies backed away from the stricken king.

"With any luck, he's copped it," Richard hissed.

"I'm sure he has," came a soft voice from the shadows.

"Buckingham?"

The Duke of Buckingham bowed. "England needs someone in charge who's far stronger than Edward, your grace. Who knows … it might even be someone like you."

"You think so?" said Richard.

"Why not? And you could be in charge, I fancy … especially with a little help from someone like me."

"And what would this help of yours cost?"

"Shall we say the vacant castle and lands of the Earl of Hereford?"

Richard cocked his head. He squinted over his lump of a shoulder at the tall, elegant man who loomed over him. Did Richard's eyes flash a moment in jealousy? Or was this just a trick of the light? "Let's talk," he said.

Only one other person in the room noticed the sudden exit of both dukes – the first of them as bent as a bow and the second as straight as a pikestaff. Mad Queen Margaret, of course, noticed everything. She smiled a sour, world-weary smile. "So, now it's *two* pigs with their snouts in the trough. Oh, they're sure to prosper for a while as villains always do. But mark my words, Richard. The day will come soon enough when I'll see your bones splinter and rot in a grave of your own foul making – "

Margaret had laid her famous curse on him.

5 Black Patch and Red Hair

There was a clip-clop of horses' hooves on the cobbles. An open carriage, hung with flags and pennants, was crossing a huddled square of houses close to the Tower of London. Sprawled across the passenger seat was a bored-looking, scrunched-up mess of a man.

"That's Crookback Dick!" whispered a red-haired chestnut seller, lifting his gaze from his stall.

Black Patch, an old soldier, gave a snort. "That's the Lord Protector of England, you mean."

"Since when?"

"Since King Edward died last week. The Lord Protector's job is to look after the royal princes while they're still kids – Prince Edward and his little brother, Prince Richard. Their uncle, Crookback Dick, is in charge for now … till Prince Edward's old enough to become king."

"You think that'll ever happen?" said Red Hair.

"Fat chance."

Heads down so they didn't seem to be snooping, the two men watched the carriage clatter over the tower's drawbridge and disappear through the arch of its fortress-thick entrance. Red Hair shivered. "I wonder what he's doing in that stink-hole of a place!"

"Tormenting some of the poor souls he's locked up, I expect. To make sure their stay isn't too long."

"You mean … he's going to kill them?"

"That's exactly what I mean."

Black Patch drew a finger across his throat. "Lord Rivers is in there, they reckon. So's Lord Grey and Lord Dorset. All three of them are lined up for the chop is what I've heard … that's if they haven't been chopped already."

Uneasily, Red Hair poked at the glowing cinders under his tray of chestnuts.

"How do you know all this stuff?"

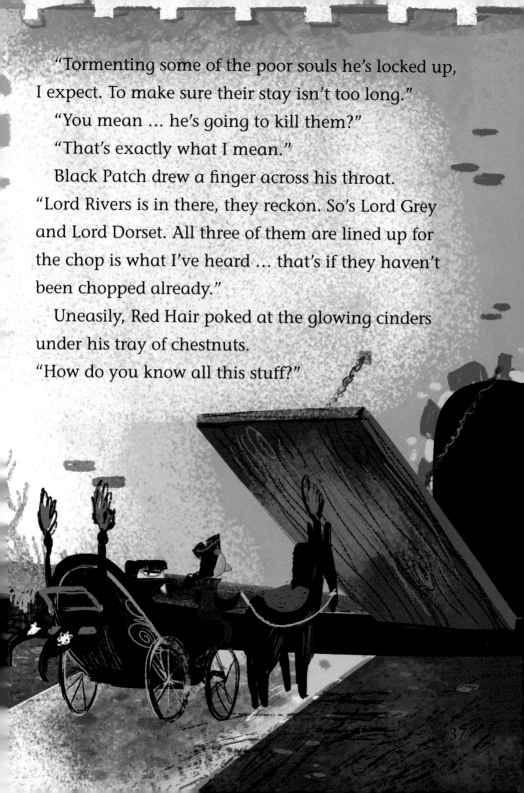

The old soldier tapped his nose. "Got a mate who serves at table. These high and mighty types who live in castles and palaces think servants are blind, deaf and dumb. There's not much a good waiter misses, though. According to my mate, the red rose of York may have duffed up the white rose of Lancaster but now they're busy duffing each other up like rats in a sack. They all want to be Top Rat, you see. Especially himself with the hump. Wouldn't trust him as far as I could throw him, that one."

"I've heard he – "

"Shush!"

38

More hoof-beats, and a rattle of harness, echoed through the archway, over the drawbridge and across the cobblestones of the square. There were two passengers in the coach now. One of them was as smooth and handsome as the other was squat and ugly. "Crookback Dick again," whispered Red Hair. "But who's his friend?"

"Buckingham," said Black Patch. "All the charm in the world, he's got. And a lot of the harm, too."

"They're stopping!" Red Hair yelped.

To his dismay, the carriage had come to a halt.

Richard beckoned with his claw of a hand.
In the early morning gloom, he looked like a crumpled
crow who'd had a serious tiff with a windmill.

"Good fellow!" he piped up.

"My lord?"

"Some of your very best chestnuts, if you please.
My companion here was up at dawn today … to finish
off some urgent business. It's left him rather peckish.
Isn't that right, your grace?"

"Just a bit," Buckingham smiled.

"At once, my lord," Red Hair stammered. "At once."

But it wasn't quite at once. Twice he spilt hot
chestnuts over the cobbles as he fumbled them into
a bag. In the end, all fingers and thumbs himself,
Black Patch had to help him.

Neither Richard nor Buckingham were bothered. Whatever had gone on in the tower this morning, so early and so urgent, must've been a huge success. Suddenly, between munches, Buckingham lifted a finger. "Gentlemen," he said, "can you spare us a moment?"

"Of course, your grace."

"Come closer."

Red Hair and Black Patch exchanged a glance. Nervously, they edged towards the carriage.

"Closer than that," snapped Buckingham. "You want the whole world to hear us?" He began to whisper.

The chestnut seller and the old soldier listened intently. Even then they could hardly believe what they'd heard. "Is that all?" blinked the chestnut seller. "And we get a gold piece for doing it?"

"Each of us?" added the old soldier.

"Each of you," Buckingham nodded. "But only if you do it exactly as I've explained. No one must suspect anything. Do it wrong and you'll get a noose round your neck instead. Have I made that clear?"

"Very clear, sir – yes!"

"Clear as crystal," the old soldier saluted. "You can rely on us to do our duty for England, sir."

"I do rely on you," said Buckingham.

"And so do I," said Richard.

With a flick of the coachman's whip, the carriage moved off.

The old soldier spat in the palm of his hand as if to shine up his gold piece. The chestnut seller fingered his neck as if to soothe the mark of a rope. "Don't even consider crossing them," said Black Patch. "Not a pair like that."

"You think I'm daft?" said Red Hair, with a gulp.

6 Princes and more plotting

The young princes had arrived at the royal palace.

And why not?

As the sons of the dead King Edward they were next in line to the throne. The elder son, Prince Edward, would be king one day, and his little brother Prince Richard was ... well, a spare heir in case of accident. But what accident could possibly happen to two small boys living in such luxury?

Their Uncle Richard, that's what.

Richard was an expert in accidents ... mainly of the "on-purpose" kind. The royal palace was tricky even for him, though. He set to work on the problem at once. "Safety," he told the boys. "That's the most important thing. I've got to make things safe for both of you."

"Aren't we safe here, Uncle?"

"Not yet, your majesty," said Richard with a sigh.

"Your highness, you mean," said Prince Edward. "I'm not 'your majesty' till I've been crowned."

Richard smiled his thinnest smile. "But you will be soon enough, dear nephew. It's my chief duty as Lord Protector to shield the two of you from risk. This palace is royal, yes. But it's also very public. People come here from all over the kingdom. Every nook and cranny must be checked, must be guarded, must be *fortified*. Till that's done, I need somewhere much stronger and more secure for you. Somewhere like … like – "

"Like the Tower of London?" Prince Richard giggled.

"What did you say?"

"The Tower of London, Uncle. I was only joking – "

"That's brilliant!"

"But Uncle – "

"So young and yet so wise," said Richard, rolling his eyes in admiration. "The Tower of London never entered my head. Yet it tripped off your tongue so readily. What it is to have such a fresh young brain!"

"Uncle!"

It was too late to protest.

Already Richard was calling for servants to pack their baggage, for the royal coach to transport them, for guards to watch every inch of their journey across the city.

"How long will you keep them in the tower?" asked Buckingham a little later when he heard the news.

"Oh … no longer than *forever*."

Buckingham laughed. He cut it short when he saw the gleam in Richard's eye. "Of course," he said, hastily. "Good plan."

"Speaking of good plans," said Richard.

"My lord?"

"Have you set up our little trap for Lord Hastings? The man's a fool, I know. But he's a powerful fool who can still make trouble for us. You've got everything prepared for this morning's meeting, have you? All the paperwork's signed and sealed to look genuine?"

"Every last word," said Buckingham.

"Come, then. Let's make a little more mischief," said Richard. "So far today, we've been on a winning streak."

"And will be still, I promise."

"You'd better hope so," said Richard, drily.

How could he move so fast on legs that looked far too spindly to carry a back as bulky and bent as his was? Despite his height and his trim figure, Buckingham had to trot to keep up.

In the grand council chamber of the palace, Richard's advisers were chatting amongst themselves while they waited. Was Richard going to be late? He was never late, was he? Unless, that is, he chose to be.

Lord Stanley, till now the crown's most trusted soldier, shifted his seat a little closer to Lord Hastings, Richard's most *trusting* soldier. "So you're not worried about all these recent … er … events?" he asked in a low voice.

"Not at all. Are you?"

"A bit, yes."

"Nonsense!" Hastings laughed. "Remember, I know Richard of old. I've been his dearest friend for years. Like two peas in a pod, we are. He loves me like a brother."

"Like Edward and George, you mean? Not very lucky with brothers, is he?"

Hastings scratched his head. He wasn't a man for deep thinking. Or for thinking of any kind come to that. "Just a run of bad luck," he shrugged. "Could've happened to anyone."

"So you're not afraid you'll be part of the bad luck?"

"Not a chance."

"We need take no precautions, then?"

"Precautions against Richard? Me? I'm not like you, Stanley. I don't snuffle about with my nose to the ground looking for plots and skulduggery. Keep things simple, that's my advice."

Lord Stanley sat back in his chair. In his experience, simplicity and Richard seldom went together. He'd realised long ago that if you weren't one step ahead of him, Richard was at least two steps ahead of you. "Let's hope you're right, Hastings," he murmured, "for the sake of all of us."

This time, Richard made a different entrance. No flinging open of doors, as usual, no clumsy strut across the room like some emperor of all the world's invalids. Instead, as everyone shuffled to their feet, he ushered in Buckingham first. Richard's face drooped with disappointment. He sidled to his own seat at the council table as if reluctant to be there at all. "Sit, my good lords," he said in a hushed voice.

He greeted each one of them with a shy smile.

Except Hastings.

Hastings, it seemed, was invisible. He stayed invisible while Richard spread a sheaf of papers over the table top, lined up every sheet with his fingertips, and gave the tiniest, saddest glance – one after another – to everyone watching him. Well, almost everyone watching him.

Still not Hastings.

The smiling dandy of a man shifted, uneasily.
He wasn't *that* stupid. He could sense something
was wrong. He just couldn't work out what it was
and why it should involve himself of all people.
He coughed, politely. "Is something troubling you,
my lord?" he asked.

"Troubling me?"

Richard seemed to uncoil like a snake big enough
to swallow a stag in one mouthful – horns, hooves
and all. "Troubling me?" he repeated. "I'm so glad
you asked that, Lord Hastings. In fact, you're just
the person to answer a question for me, if you please."

"Gladly," said Hastings, perking up.

"Tell me, then. Suppose an old, old friend, a comrade-in-arms, a member of the highest council in the land, were to betray the leader who'd relied upon him all his life? To commit treachery, in short. What fate would a fellow like that deserve, Lord Hastings?"

"Deserve?" Hastings gave a growl of relief that his answer could be so easy. "Death, my lord!" he thundered. "Instant death! The block, the axe, the axeman ... and ... and – "

"All the trimmings?"

"Why not?"

"Why not indeed?" Richard said.

He shuffled the papers on the table top.

"All the evidence is here, my lords. Every detail, from every witness, gathered so carefully by our good servant, the Duke of Buckingham. It breaks my heart to say it after all these years, but you're the traitor, Lord Hastings."

"Me?"

"Yes, *you.*"

Richard paused to choke back a sob. "So let me follow the excellent advice you've always given me in the past. What was it you said? Instant death? By way of the block, the axe, the axeman? No man of honour could possibly disagree. But that isn't all, of course – "

"It isn't?" squeaked Hastings in relief.

Richard was looking straight at him now as his lipless slit of a mouth delivered its verdict. "As you rightly reminded me, my lord, we mustn't forget *all the trimmings.*"

The royal council was rigid with shock. Nobody moved and nobody spoke. The only sound to be heard was a hollow, rasping rattle in the throat of the man who'd just been condemned.

7 Richard opens his purse

It isn't easy to steal a kingdom from its rightful ruler.
By now, though, England was thoroughly unsettled
and ready for a strong new king to take over – Richard
had seen to that. First, who hadn't heard the gossip
about that scary old baggage Mad Queen Margaret?
What with her swearing and cursing – enough to freeze
anyone's blood – surely there had to be some truth in
her complaints about the violent deaths in her family?

Second came the mysterious disappearances.
Who was the latest lord or earl or duke to have
vanished from sight? People didn't dare think about it.
The answer was too depressing.

Third were the rumours
about these so-called young
"princes". Were they *really*
princes? people asked.
Or had someone smuggled
a pair of imposters into
the palace? All this doubt
and uncertainty played
straight into Richard's hands.

Altogether, conditions were perfect for Richard and Buckingham to make their bid for power. All they needed was the right time, the right place and the right person to tip public opinion in their favour. Soon, they'd set up a plot which covered all three: the time – early morning; the place – Richard's courtyard; the person – his worship, the Lord Mayor of London.

Buckingham laid a respectful hand on the arm of the Lord Mayor. "My lord," he said, "I hear what you're saying about this constant battle for power between the House of York and the House of Lancaster. I hear the same thing everywhere I go in town or country. It's like some dreary song I can't shake out of my head."

"So what's the answer, your grace?"

The mayor was a plump, simpering man who longed to be a duke himself. Buckingham eyed him shrewdly. "That's why I asked you to meet me here – you and these honourable citizens of yours."

"My followers, yes," said the mayor, smugly.

All round him, people jostled each other impatiently. Why had the Lord Mayor summoned them? This was the Duke of Gloucester's courtyard, wasn't it? What had Crookback Dick got to do with it?

"Ah – " said Buckingham, as if he'd read their minds. "Here comes the very man to solve our problems. It's Richard, our Lord Protector, just as I expected."

He pointed at a balcony above them.

Richard had staged another of his entrances. Right on cue, he'd swept back a curtain and hobbled out into the sunlight. Perhaps it was too bright for him, though. He didn't seem to notice that the Lord Mayor, and half the city of London, was gawping up at him.

Well, *nearly* half the city of London. At any rate, that's how it felt as everyone craned their necks to get the best view. Immediately, they gasped in surprise. Behind Richard came a line of beggars – tatty, rackety and sick – with begging bowls clutched in their hands. They formed an orderly queue across the balcony as if they'd done this many times before. "Every Thursday," remarked Buckingham. "Richard calls it his giving day."

"Every Thursday, you say?"

"Never misses."

A hush had fallen over the courtyard. You could hear the clink of a coin in every bowl as Richard moved along the line with his leather purse.

He looked like an old black raven sharing its titbits. Not a pretty sight.

But the beggars were too grateful and too hungry to shrink away from him. They bowed and curtsied politely as he passed. And Richard bowed back at each of them as if they themselves were lords and ladies.

It was his masterstroke.

Afterwards, nobody was quite sure when the murmuring began. To begin with, it was just a voice or two in the crowd. Then came a chanting and a stamping of feet. Quickly, this swelled into a shout of approval: "Richard for king! Richard for king! Richard for king!"

"Richard for king!" the Lord Mayor bleated.

Buckingham gave a helpless shrug. "Your supporters are as wise as you are, my lord," he purred. "It's obvious what they want. And who could possibly deny such a request?"

Not the Lord Mayor, certainly.

Not now half the city of London – or so it appeared – had made up its mind what the nation needed. By the time the other half of London had caught up, along with the rest of England, nobody would've guessed how the uproar started. Two men only had launched it – one of them with red hair that smelt of chestnuts, and the other with a black patch over his left eye.

8 King Richard III

Alone in the palace throne room, Richard's glance
fell on his shadow. It was barely visible in the shifting
firelight but he could still make out his hump,
his hand and his oddly turned-in feet.

Also, he could see the crown on his head.

Richard smiled. "The crown of England," he said.
"Mine at last for as long as I live – " He paused.

How long would that be?

Winning a crown was
one thing. Keeping it
was quite another.
Of all people,
he'd good reason
to know that.
Was there anyone
he could really trust?
Besides, did trusting
anyone really matter?
Wasn't it better by far
to be one jump in front
of any challenger?

He heard the swish of a tapestry and the creak of a door opening. "You sent for me, your majesty?" called Buckingham.

"We have unfinished business, my lord."

"We have," the duke agreed. He mounted the steps to the throne and knelt before his royal master.

"With the princes," Richard went on.

"The princes?"

"I must be rid of them both. While they have breath in their bodies, how can I breathe freely in mine? They're a threat, Buckingham – a reminder to my enemies that they've a claim to the throne more lawful than mine. You see that?"

"But they're locked in the tower – "

Richard's eyes glittered. "Buckingham, anyone can be locked in the tower. Anyone at all."

Buckingham stiffened and rose to his feet. "Let me think it through," he said. "You took me by surprise."

"Did I? Then your wits must be getting slower. What was the unfinished business *you* were thinking of?"

"Your majesty – "

"Tell me."

"Hereford, your majesty. You promised me the castle and its estates if I helped you with your … your life's ambition."

"So I did."

The newly-crowned King of England sat back on his newly-won throne. He lifted a hand – his bad hand – and fluttered it in the air. "Is this a Thursday, Buckingham?" he asked.

"A Thursday?"

"No, it isn't. So I'm not in my giving mood today. Perhaps I never will be again … who knows? I've had the stench of those beggars in my nostrils ever since. Oh, there's a rough fellow named Tyrell waiting outside. As you leave, would you kindly ask him to come in?"

Buckingham's face darkened. Was he about to speak? If so, he thought better of it.

"As it pleases your majesty," he bowed.

Richard's meeting with Tyrell was short. All it involved was handing over a bunch of keys and repeating some strict instructions. No dagger and no water butt in this case, Tyrell agreed. If held down firmly enough, a pillow over both the princes' faces should be all that was needed.

Richard may have achieved his life's ambition but he was still as sharp and focused as ever.

His wits hadn't slowed down one bit.

9 A step too far

So what could possibly go wrong?

Good question.

Surely a run of luck like Richard's couldn't last for ever. He'd miss a few telltale signs of danger, wouldn't he? Or rush things just a little too much? Then again, maybe the sheer thrill of plotting would ruin him. Take his new queen, Anne, for instance. Suppose she were to fall sick … was there anyone else around who'd make him a more *useful* wife?

Richard was so wrapped up in his trickery, he didn't hear what Lord Stanley had told him. "Buckingham?" he snapped. "That snivelling faint-heart? What about him?"

"He's fled, your majesty."

"Fled?"

"To the north, they say. He's using his money
and his influence over other nobles to raise an army
against you – "

"He's attacking me from the north?"

"From the north, yes."

Lord Stanley lowered his eyes and looked away.
Richard picked up on this at once. He tilted forward
on his throne like a vulture perched on a crag.
"And what about the south?" he asked.

"The south, your majesty?
Nobody in the south of England – "

"Who mentioned England, my lord? I'm thinking more southerly than that. *France* is the place I have in mind. You've a son-in-law there, I believe … Lord Richmond. On holiday, is he? Or is he perhaps gathering an army to attack me from across the channel?"

The colour had drained from Lord Stanley's face. "Your majesty!" he protested. "Never in all my life have I betrayed my king!"

"I know it, Stanley. The whole world knows how honest you are and how faithful. And I intend to keep it that way. Am I right in saying you've another son in your family whose name is – ?"

"George."

67

"George, yes. It's amazing how often these Georges crop up. Well, your son George is on holiday too."

"Is he?"

"As an honoured guest of my own. I'm keeping him safe in the tower, you see – safe as a bug in a rug. Trust me on that. Think of it as a little reward for his father's famous loyalty to his king."

Richard held Stanley's gaze a moment – a long probing moment – and Stanley saw murder in his eyes. It was a lesson he never forgot. Here was a man at his most dangerous when you thought he was losing his grip.

10 The Battle of Bosworth

Yet still Richard's luck was on a roll. News came that Buckingham had been captured and killed. Even better, fierce storms had scattered the ships bringing Richmond and his army to England.

Richard was delighted.

If a shadow could smile, his would've been beaming.

He checked maps, totted up numbers and considered the situation from every angle. But perhaps it was boredom, as much as tactics, which drove him to action.

"There's no better moment than this," he yawned. "By the time Richmond's rescued his fleet, and landed his men on shore, my army will be twice the size of his. Why, I'll smash him to smithereens. Has he forgotten my record as a fighting man?"

As a fighting man, Richard was at his best. With a helmet to lift his head, armour to prop him up, and clamps at elbow and knee to hold him steady, he seemed almost normal – a match for anyone kitted out for battle. Even his waddle of a walk had a cut-and-thrust look to it.

On horseback, he was a giant.

So, when his army and Richmond's finally faced each other in battle across Bosworth field, Richard announced that victory was his for the taking. "I'm your king," he told his troops. "Never forget that."

Richmond was more modest. "From tomorrow, I may be your king," he told *his* troops. "If I am, then I promise you'll bless the day you made it possible."

That night, on the eve of battle, Richmond slept the calm, untroubled sleep of a young man who fears dishonour much more than defeat. This wasn't so with Richard. Dishonour meant nothing to him and defeat was a notion he'd rejected from the day he was born. "It's a word for weaklings," he declared. "Not fit for the lips of a true warrior."

71

He ran a finger along the blade of his favourite sword to check its keenness. "As for *death*," he went on, "that's a word I can respect … as long as it's me who's dishing it out."

It was his last thought before he closed his eyes.

Maybe that explains Richard's dreams.

Death appeared in every one of them. George, stabbed and sopping wet, was first. King Edward came next, doomed by the royal pardon he'd sent too late.

Five noblemen followed – all beheaded on the block.

Finally, two young princes made their appearance … smothered under the same pillow.

Richard woke up in a fury. "Plagued by nightmares tonight of all nights?" he snarled. "What monstrosity is this?"

"Your majesty!" a messenger was shouting. "The enemy is upon us! They've charged an hour before sunrise! And Lord Stanley's with them leading an army of his own!"

"Lord Stanley?" Richard shrieked. "Then his son George must pay for it! Off with his head!"

"After the battle, your majesty?"

"Of course, after the battle! We've enough to attend to right now, you fool.
To arms, everyone!
Everyone to arms!"

Once he'd been hoisted into the saddle, Richard was magnificent. In those days, remember, fighting was up close and personal – just the way he liked it. Blade or battle-axe, spear or dagger – whatever weapon he faced – he simply swept his opponent aside as if swatting at flies not men. Everywhere he galloped, he left a trail of blood. "I've killed five Richmond lookalikes already!" his reedy voice rang out. "When will the real one dare confront me?"

Some say Richard would've vanquished Richmond's army single-handed if he could've fought them one-by-one. Even in clusters, they reeled back in terror at the savagery of his attacks.

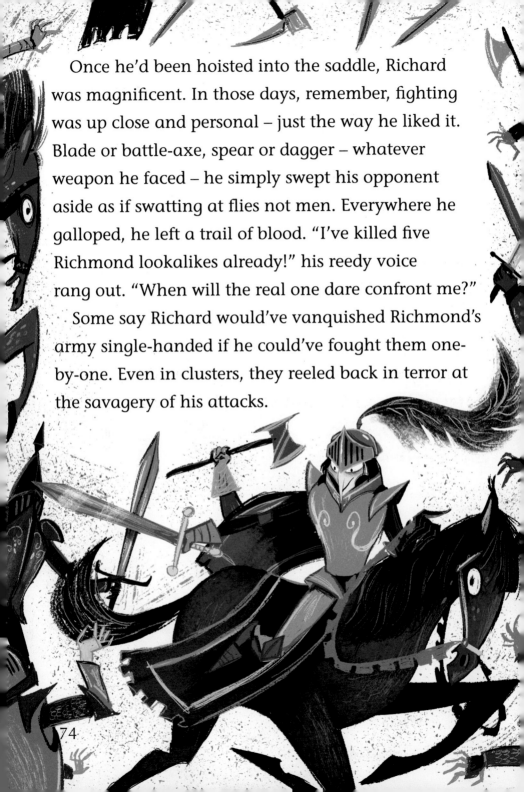

Then disaster struck.

The stallion he was riding stumbled and fell dead. Dazed, Richard staggered to his feet. He knew at once everything had changed. A man on foot, in full armour, is very different from a man who's mounted. "A horse," he shrieked. "A horse! My kingdom for a horse!"

"No horse to spare," growled a man-at-arms, edging forwards.

"No kingdom, either," said another man, grimly.

"And soon no Richard," added a third.

Already Richard was surrounded. Even then, he refused to yield. Thrusting, slashing, parrying, his sword kept them cringing away from him time after time. When Richmond number six arrived to finish him off – the real Richmond this time – he was still spitting defiance.

That was the end of it.

Later, everyone agreed that Richard, and what was left of his famous shadow, went on twitching long after his body lay lifeless.

"The dog is dead at last," Richmond said, with a shudder.

"And you are King Henry VII of England," said Stanley. "Here … take the crown, your majesty. You won it fair and square."

"But not without cost, I fear. How's your son George?"

"Still safe in the tower."

"Praise be."

The new king was scanning the battlefield. What soldiers call "the mopping up" had already begun. As far as the eye could see, the wounded were being tended, graves were being dug and fires were being lit for feasting. A wind was lifting the grass on the lower slopes. If you listened hard, you could hear the gentle swish of it.

Or maybe it wasn't so gentle.

Some people, perhaps those who listened hardest, said it couldn't help reminding them of a mad old queen called Margaret who was whispering "told-you-so, told-you-so, told-you-so," under her breath.

Richard's diary: 21st August 1485

Well, it's finally come – the moment I've plotted and schemed for all my life. I've managed to get rid of all the people who stood in my way – George, Edward, a troublesome rabble of noblemen, even my young nephews – and now only one thing stands between me and my destiny. After tomorrow's battle, no one will be able to question my right to be king!

The Battle of Bosworth will go down in history as the day that I – King Richard III – finally defeated the snivelling wretches who've always tried to put me down. I can hardly wait to see the look in their eyes when I – the crook-backed King of England – dispatch their lives with my sword!

Thoughts of my victory are whirling round in my head already. That dog Richmond will struggle to sleep tonight, I'm sure! But I won't – I've never had a nightmare in my life, and I'm not about to start now. No, the dead will stay sleeping, where they belong, and tomorrow, I'll secure my claim to the throne of England – for ever!

Richard III

Ideas for reading

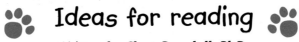

Written by Clare Dowdall, PhD
Lecturer and Primary Literacy Consultant

Reading objectives:
- draw inferences such as inferring characters' feelings, thoughts and motives from their actions, and justify inferences with evidence
- discuss and evaluate how authors use language, including figurative language, considering the impact on the reader
- provide reasoned justifications for their views

Spoken language objectives:
- ask relevant questions to extend their understanding and knowledge
- select and use appropriate registers for effective communication

Curriculum links: History – British monarchs; Art – drawing

Resources: paper and art materials for drawing

Build a context for reading
- Explain that *Richard III* is an historical play by William Shakespeare.
- Look at the front cover and discuss what clues the illustrator is providing about Richard's character.
- Read the blurb together and brainstorm adjectives to describe what can be inferred about Richard's character, e.g. he's ruthless, ambitious, determined.

Understand and apply reading strategies
- Turn to the character list on pp2–3. Work together to create a web to show how the characters are related. Show children how to annotate each character with information that can be deduced from the illustrations.
- Turn to pp4–6. Ask a volunteer to read the text aloud. Challenge children to collect descriptive words and phrases that paint a picture of Richard.